KING EUGENE'S WASHING MACHINE

Written by RE Beckum
Illustrated by Alyssa Beckum

◆ FriesenPress

Suite 300 - 990 Fort St
Victoria, BC, V8V 3K2
Canada

www.friesenpress.com

ISBN
978-1-5255-8445-9 (Hardcover)
0978-1-5255-8446-6 (Paperback)
978-1-5255-8447-3 (eBook)

1. JUVENILE FICTION, STORIES IN VERSE

Distributed to the trade by The Ingram Book Company

KING EUGENE'S
WASHING MACHINE

Written by RE Beckum
illustrated by Alyssa Beckum

There once was a king named Eugene
Who was married to Queen Bernadine
Their children were wild
But they loved every child
Dean, Gene, Irene, and Jolene

Although King Eugene and his queen
Had four children, it seemed like fifteen

They loved watching them play
In their wild, wacky way
The problem was getting them clean

Dean, Gene, Irene, and Jolene
Had a delightful daily routine
They ate breakfast in bed:
Two slices of bread
With butter and jam in between...

Then they'd gulp down their milk in a flash
Which gave each a milky mustache
Their hands would be sticky
And feel really icky
But right out the door they would dash

One morning, Queen Bernadine
Packed a picnic for Dean, Gene, Irene, and Jolene

She took the whole bunch
To the lake to have lunch
And she slathered them all with sunscreen

Queen Bernadine said, "Now, play as you please."
So, they climbed on the rocks and the trees
They ate tons of wild berries
And sour red cherries
And were stained from their cheeks to their knees

They rolled around in the grass and the dirt
Got big stains on their shorts and their shirts
They got mud in their hair
But they just didn't care
It's a wonder they didn't get hurt

They ate pickles
and cans of sardines
Watermelon, cucumbers,
and greens
They had bread
and tomatoes
And boiled red potatoes
And spaghetti
with mashed jellybeans

They had noodles
with fried eggs and beans,
A lunch like you
never have seen
But they liked it a lot
And it just hit the spot
For Dean, Gene,
Irene and Jolene

They got back to the castle that night
And were an unbelievable sight
They were grimy and greasy
And all feeling queasy
Just like you'd imagine they might

When their dad, King Eugene, saw the mess
He did not love his kids any less
He just opened the door
He had seen this before
There was no need for worry or stress

The king took a long look at the scene
Then he said, "We must get you kids clean!
I know what we need,
Soap, and water, and speed!
In my super-cool washing machine!"

They stared with their mouths open wide
It looked like an amusement-park ride
Like a wet rollercoaster
Attached to a toaster
With a swing, and big loops, and a slide

He poured in water, soap, and shampoo
Then a bucket of bubble bath, too
Then the kids all jumped in
And they started to spin
Yelling, "Yahoo!!"
and "Wee!!"
and "Woohoo!!"

They splashed, and they sang like a choir
As the water got higher and higher
Then they slid down the slide
That dropped them inside
King Eugene's warm and toasty "kid dryer"

King Eugene smiled and said to his queen,
"That's the wildest thing I've ever seen.
Those kids were so grimy,
So filthy and slimy,
Now they all have a bright, shiny sheen!"

21

Dean, Gene, Irene, and Jolene
Came out all sweet-smelling and clean
The part they loved most?
When they popped out like toast
All cozy and warm and pristine

When they landed in bed in a heap
Queen Bernadine heard not a peep
And with hair that was puffy
And clothes that were fluffy
They fell into a sweet, dreamy sleep.

There once was a king named Eugene
Who was married to Queen Bernadine
Their children were wild
But they loved every child
Dean, Gene, Irene, and Jolene

R.E. BECKUM
AUTHOR

R.E. (Randell) Beckum has four fine adult children who were playful and wild and inspiring. He also has three fine grandchildren who are happily following in the same family tradition. He lives in Hawaii with his wife, Queen Florence, and twelve papaya trees.

ALYSSA BECKUM
ILLUSTRATOR

Alyssa Beckum is an artist and illustrator currently based in Kansas City. She is the youngest of the author's four fine adult children. She loves baking bread and bathes regularly using a normal washing machine.

9 781525 584466